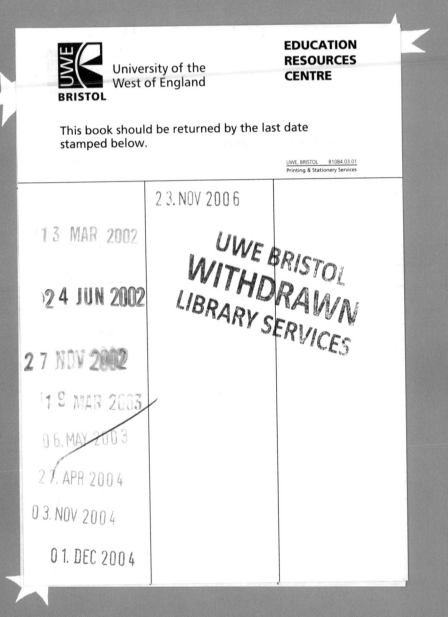

For Will

LILLY'S PURPLE PLASTIC PURSE
by Kevin Henkes
British Library Cataloguing in Publication Data
A catalogue record of this book is available from the British Library

ISBN 0 340 714646 (HB)
ISBN 0 340 714654 (PB)

Text and illustrations copyright © Kevin Henkes 1996

The right of Kevin Henkes to be identified as author
of this work has been asserted by her in accordance
with the Copyright, Design and Patents Act 1988

First US edition published in 1996
by Greenwillow Books,
a division of William Morrow & Company Inc.,
New York, United States of America

First UK edition published in 1998
by Hodder Children's Books,
a division of Hodder Headline plc,
338 Euston Road, London NW1 3BH

10 9 8 7 6 5 4 3 2 1

Printed in Belgium

Y
School stories
CF

Lilly's Purple Plastic Purse

By Kevin Henkes

Hodder
Children's
Books

A division of Hodder Headline plc

LILLY loved school.

She loved the pointy pencils.

She loved the squeaky chalk.

And she loved the way her boots
went clickety-clickety-click
down the long, shiny hallways.

Lilly loved the privacy
of her very own desk.

She loved the fish fingers.
and chocolate milk
every Friday
in the dining room.

And, most of all,
she loved her teacher,
Mr Slinger.

Mr Slinger was as bright as a button.

He wore artistic shirts.

He wore glasses on a chain round his neck.

And he wore a different coloured tie
for each day of the week.

"Wow," said Lilly. That was just about all she could say. "Wow."

Instead of "Greetings, students,"
or "Good morning, pupils,"
Mr Slinger winked and said, "Howdy!"

He thought that desks in rows
were old-fashioned and boring.
"Do you rodents think you
can handle a semicircle?"

And he always provided
the most tasty snacks -
things that were curly
and crunchy and cheesy.

"I want to be a teacher
when I grow up," said Lilly.
"Me too!" said her friends
Chester and Wilson and Victor.

At home Lilly pretended to be Mr Slinger.
"I am the teacher," she told her baby brother, Julius. "Righto!"
Lilly even wanted her own set of deluxe picture encyclopedias.

"What's up with Lilly?" asked her mother.
"I thought she wanted to be a surgeon or an ambulance driver
or a diva," said her father.
"It must be because of her new teacher, Mr Slinger," said her mother.
"Wow," said her father. That was just about all he could say. "Wow."

Whenever the students had free time, they were allowed to go
to the Lightbulb Lab in the back of the classroom.
They expressed their ideas creatively through drawing and writing.
Lilly went often.
She had a lot of ideas.
She drew pictures of Mr Slinger.
And she wrote stories about him too.
During Show-and-Tell, Lilly showed her creations to the entire class.
"Wow," said Mr Slinger. That was just about all he could say. "Wow."

AND AT THE
VERY LAST SECOND —
MR SLINGER
SAVED THE COLD,
STARVING,
ELDERLY...

When Mr Slinger had bus duty,
Lilly queued up even though
she didn't go on the bus.

Lilly raised her hand
more than anyone else in class
(even if she didn't know the answer).

And she volunteered to stay
after school to clap blackboard
rubbers.

"I want to be a teacher
when I grow up," said Lilly.
"Excellent choice," said Mr Slinger.

One Monday morning Lilly came to school especially happy.
She had gone shopping with her granny over the weekend.
Lilly had a new pair of film star sunglasses, complete with
glittery diamonds and a chain like Mr Slinger's.
She had three shiny pound coins.
And, best of all, she had a brand new purple plastic purse
that played a jaunty tune when it was opened.

Lilly wanted to show everyone.

"Not now," said Mr Slinger.

"Listen to our story."

Lilly had a hard time listening.

SHHH —

Lilly *really* wanted to show everyone.

"Not now," said Mr Slinger.

"Let's be fair to our classmates."

Lilly had a hard time being fair.

mice
nice
rice
dice

— LICE

Lilly really, really wanted to show everyone.

"Not now," said Mr Slinger.

"Wait until playtime or Show-and-Tell."

But Lilly could not wait.

TYPES OF CHEESE
SWISS
CHEDDAR
BRIE
MOZZARELLA

SHE'S IN TROUBLE.

The glasses were so glittery.
The coins were so shiny.
And the purse played such
nice music, not to mention
how excellent it was for
storing school supplies.

"Look," Lilly whispered fiercely.
"Look, everyone. Look what I've got!"
Everyone looked.
Including Mr Slinger.
He was not amused.

"I'll just keep your things on my desk until the end of the day," said Mr Slinger. "They'll be safe there, and then you can take them home."

Lilly's stomach lurched.
She felt like crying.
Her glasses were gone.
Her coins were gone.
Her purple plastic purse was gone.
Lilly longed for her purse all morning.
She was even too sad to eat the snack
Mr Slinger served before playtime.

That afternoon Lilly went to the Lightbulb Lab.

She was still very sad.

She thought and she thought and she thought.

And then she became angry.

She thought and she thought and she thought some more.

And then she became furious.

She thought and she thought and she thought a bit longer.

And then she drew a picture of Mr Slinger.

Just before the last bell rang, Lilly sneaked the drawing into Mr Slinger's book-bag.

When all the students were buttoned and zipped and snapped
and tied and ready to go home, Mr Slinger strolled over to
Lilly and gave her purple plastic purse back.

"It's a beautiful purse," said Mr Slinger. "Your coins are nice
and jingly. And those glasses are absolutely fabulous. You may
bring them back to school as long as you don't disturb the rest
of the class."

"I do not want to be a teacher when I grow up," Lilly said
as she marched out of the classroom.

On the way home Lilly opened her purse.
Her glasses and coins were inside.
And so was a note from Mr Slinger. It said:
"Today was a difficult day.
Tomorrow will be better."
There was also a bag of tasty snacks
at the bottom of the purse.

Lilly's stomach lurched.
She felt like crying.
She felt simply awful.

Lilly ran all the way home and told her mother and father everything.

Instead of watching her favourite cartoons, Lilly decided to sit in the uncooperative chair.

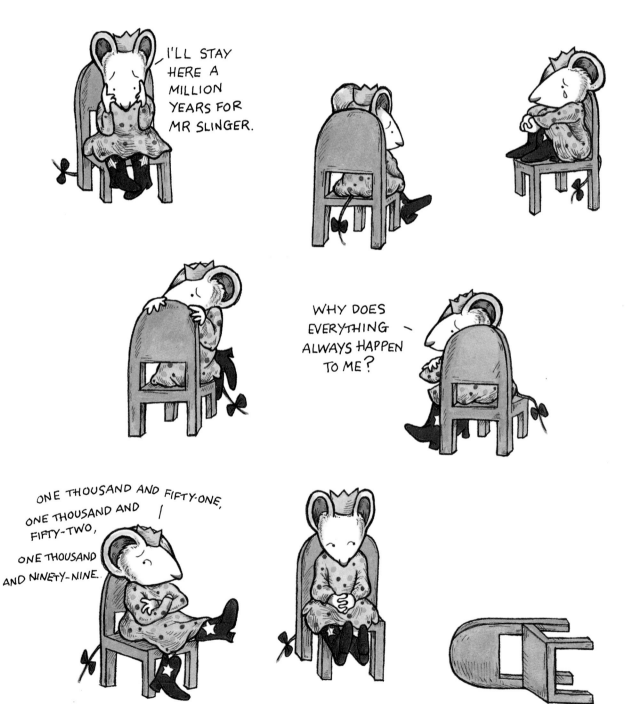

That night Lilly drew a new picture of Mr Slinger
and wrote a story about him too.

Lilly was really really Sorry.

So everyone forgave her.

Even her parents.

Even her stinky baby brother.

Even her especially incredible teacher.

And then the sun shined its smiley face down on everyone and everything.
Even the beetles and worms.

THE END

Righto!!!
I forgive Everyone!!!

Kind Good Nice

←could be head teacher

~I am really really really really really really really really SORRY!!!

LILLY

worms ↓

beetles →

←oops

I'M AN AUTHOR!

Lilly's mother wrote a note.
And Lilly's father baked some tasty snacks for Lilly to take
to school the next day.
"I think Mr Slinger will understand," said Lilly's mother.
"I know he will," said Lilly's father.

The next morning Lilly got to school early.

"These are for you," Lilly said to Mr Slinger.

"Because I'm really, really, really, really, really, really, really, really, really, really, really, really, really, really, really, really, really, really, really, really sorry."

Mr Slinger read the story.

And he looked at the picture.

And he read the note.

And he sampled the snacks.

"Wow," said Mr Slinger.
That was just about all
he could say. "Wow."

"What do you think we should do with this?" asked Mr Slinger.
"Could we just throw it away?" asked Lilly.
"Excellent idea," said Mr Slinger.

During Show-and-Tell, Lilly demonstrated the many uses and
unique qualities of her purple plastic purse, her shiny coins,
and her glittery, film star sunglasses.

Then she did a little performance using them as props.
"It's called Interpretive Dance," said Lilly.
Mr Slinger joined in.
"Wow," said the entire class. That was just about all
they could say. "Wow."

Throughout the rest of the day, Lilly's purse and coins
and sunglasses were tucked safely inside her desk.
She peeked at them often but did not disturb a soul.

Just before the last bell rang, Mr Slinger served Lilly's snacks,
to everyone's delight.
"What do you want to be when you grow up?" asked Mr Slinger.
"A TEACHER!" everyone replied. Lilly's reply was the loudest.
"Excellent choice," said Mr Slinger.

As the pupils filed out of the classroom,
Lilly held her purple plastic purse close to her heart.
Mr Slinger was right - it *had* been a better day.

Lilly ran and skipped and hopped and flew all the way home,
she was so happy.
And she really *did* want to be a teacher when she grew up -

That is, when she didn't want to be a dancer
or a surgeon or an ambulance driver or a diva
or a pilot or a hairdresser or a scuba diver. . .